D0592376

# Let's Trade

## ALL ABOUT TRADING

Written by Kirsten Hall

Illustrated by Bev Luedecke

children's press®

**A Division of Scholastic Inc.**
New York  Toronto  London  Auckland  Sydney
Mexico City  New Delhi  Hong Kong
Danbury, Connecticut

# About the Author

Kirsten Hall, formerly an early-childhood teacher,
is a children's book editor in New York City. She has been
writing books for children since she was thirteen years old
and now has over sixty titles in print.

# About the Illustrator

Bev Luedecke enjoys life and nature in Colorado.
Her sparkling personality and artistic flair are reflected in her
creation of Beastieville, a world filled with lovable Beasties
that are sure to delight children of all ages.

Library of Congress Cataloging-in-Publication Data

Hall, Kirsten.
  Let's trade : all about trading / written by Kirsten Hall; illustrated by Bev Luedecke.
    p. cm. — (Beastieville)
  Summary: One day at the lake, the Beasties learn how much fun it can be to trade things with friends.
  ISBN 0-516-22999-0 (lib. bdg.)        0-516-25520-7 (pbk.)
  [1. Barter—Fiction. 2. Lakes—Fiction. 3. Stories in rhyme.]  I. Luedecke, Bev, ill. II. Title.
  PZ8.3.H146Let 2004
  [E]—dc22

                                        2004000115

1 2 3 4 5 6 7 8 9 10 R 13 12 11 10 09 08 07 06 05 04

# A NOTE TO PARENTS AND TEACHERS

Welcome to the world of the Beasties, where learning is FUN. In each of the charming stories in this series, the Beasties deal with character traits that every child can identify with. Each story reinforces appropriate concept skills for kindergartners and first graders, while simultaneously encouraging problem-solving skills. Following are just a few of the ways that you can help children get the most from this delightful series.

### Stories to be read and enjoyed

Encourage children to read the stories aloud. The rhyming verses make them fun to read. Then ask them to think about alternate solutions to some of the problems that the Beasties have faced or to imagine alternative endings. Invite children to think about what they would have done if they were in the story and to recall similar things that have happened to them.

### Activities reinforce the learning experience

The activities at the end of the books offer a way for children to put their new skills to work. They complement the story and are designed to help children develop specific skills and build confidence. Use these activities to reinforce skills. But don't stop there. Encourage children to find ways to build on these skills during the course of the day.

### Learning opportunities are everywhere

Use this book as a starting point for talking about how we use reading skills or math or social studies concepts in everyday life. When we search for a phone number in the telephone book and scan names in alphabetical order or check a list, we are using reading skills. When we keep score at a baseball game or divide a class into even-numbered teams, we are using math.

The more you can help children see that the skills they are learning in school really do have a place in everyday life, the more they will think of learning as something that is part of their lives, not as a chore to be borne. Plus you will be sending the important message that learning is fun.

Madeline Boskey Olsen, Ph.D.
Developmental Psychologist

3

Bee-Bop

Puddles

Slider

Wilbur

Pip & Zip

Flippet

Pooky

Mr. Rigby

We're
the
Beasties

Smudge

Toggles

Zip and Pip sit by the lake.
They are eating berry pie.

Flippet sees them sitting there.
She floats over to say hi.

"Oh, that berry pie looks good!
I wish I could have some, too.

8

Will you give that pie to me?
I will give my float to you!"

Zip and Pip look at her float.
Then they look down at their pie.

They decide to make the trade.
"Now we must go float. Goodbye!"

Great big Smudge plays by the lake.
"Zip and Pip! I love your float!

Do you want to make a trade?
I will trade for my new boat."

Zip and Pip trade for the boat.
Smudge says, "Look how fast they go!"

Smudge would like to try the float.
He is way too heavy though!

Toggles paints down by the lake.
Smudge asks her if she will trade.

"I will give you this new float.
You can give me what you made!"

Toggles thinks the float is great.
Smudge is drying in the sun.

Bee-Bop comes to join his friends.
"Wow, that float sure looks like fun!"

Bee-Bop holds his hands up high.
"Toggles, did you see my book?

Would you like to make a trade?
Float back here and take a look!"

Toggles likes the book a lot.
She loves all the art inside.

Bee-Bop really likes the float.
"Puddles, would you like a ride?"

Wilbur does not like the float.
"I will never trade with you!"

Pooky thinks the float is great.
"Bee-Bop, can you take me, too?"

"Sure," says Bee-Bop. "Here I come!"
"Wow!" says Pooky. "This is fun!

You must love this nice big float.
I sure wish that I had one!"

Bee-Bop hears what Pooky says.
"I will give my float to you!

It is always fun to trade.
But I like to give things, too!"

# COUNT THE TRADES

1. Which Beasties made trades in this story?

2. What did they trade?

3. Which trade do you think was the best?

# TRADING

Trading can be a lot of fun.

1. Why do you think people like to trade?

2. When would trading be a bad idea?

3. Have you ever traded any of your own things?

# WORD LIST

| | | | | |
|---|---|---|---|---|
| a | float | join | ride | up |
| always | floats | lake | say | want |
| all | for | like | says | way |
| and | friends | likes | see | we |
| are | fun | look | sees | what |
| art | give | looks | she | Wilbur |
| asks | go | lot | sit | will |
| at | good | love | sitting | wish |
| back | goodbye | loves | Smudge | with |
| Bee-Bop | great | made | some | would |
| berry | had | make | sun | wow |
| big | hands | me | sure | you |
| boat | have | must | take | your |
| book | he | my | that | Zip |
| but | hears | never | the | |
| by | heavy | new | their | |
| can | her | nice | them | |
| come | here | not | then | |
| comes | hi | now | there | |
| could | high | oh | they | |
| decide | his | one | things | |
| did | holds | over | thinks | |
| do | how | paints | this | |
| does | I | pie | though | |
| down | if | Pip | to | |
| drying | in | plays | Toggles | |
| eating | inside | Pooky | too | |
| fast | is | Puddles | trade | |
| Flippet | it | really | try | |